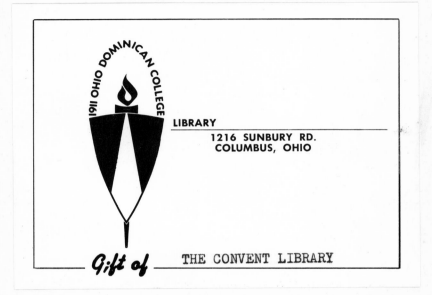

American Folk Tales are colorful tales of regional origin full of the local flavor and grass roots humor of special people and places. Coming from all areas of the United States, these stories provide entertaining reading material as well as insight into the customs and backgrounds of the regions from which they spring.

Distinctive color illustrations complement the text and add to the reader's enjoyment.

TALES
FROM NEAR-SIDE
AND FAR

BY MAY JUSTUS

DRAWINGS BY HERMAN B. VESTAL

GARRARD PUBLISHING COMPANY
CHAMPAIGN, ILLINOIS

Hound Pup Names Himself

The Tollivers lived in a little log house in the middle of No-End Hollow. Pappy was tall and lean, Mammy was short and fat, and Toby, who was going on ten, was about the right size for his age. There was also Molasses, a mule, which belonged to Pappy. He had not been named for his nature but for his coloring. Missy, the muley cow, was a great pet of Mammy's. Toby had a hound pup, but the hound pup had no name.

"A boy should name his own dog." This was

the opinion of Uncle Tobe on Yon-Side, who had given the hound pup to him. "Name that dog yourself," he had said. Then he had added, "And be certain-sure that you give him a *suitable* name!"

"A *suitable* name!" A name to suit a bouncing, mischievous puppy.

One day, Mammy caught the pup in a pot of beans, which were cooling on the hearthstone, and chased him out of the cabin. "Greedy, good-for-nothing," she took to calling him.

Pappy's pet names for the pup were "Rowdy" and "Rascal" when the dog chased Molasses in the barn lot and frightened a neighbor's team or scared the chickens off the roost. But the hound pup paid no attention, for he knew as well as anyone that he had no proper name.

"We ought to give him a suitable name before he is any older," said Toby.

"We might call him 'Worthless,'" Pappy said. "That would suit him to a *T*. All the other animals earn their board and keep. Molasses pulls the plow in the field."

"Missy gives milk," said Mammy.

"The hens lay eggs," Pappy went on. "The pigs grow fat for meat, but the hound pup does nothing but make mischief. We might as well get rid of him."

"Oh!" cried Toby, "we can't do that. It would hurt his feelings if he thought we didn't want him, and what could we do with him?"

"Take him back to Yon-Side where he came from," said Pappy. "If he doesn't mend his ways in a hip-and-hurry, that's what we'll do with him!"

So Toby took the hound pup by himself to have a little talk with him. "Listen, hound pup, you've got to learn some manners. We've got to think of things you can do to earn your board and keep."

"Boo-oo!" agreed the hound pup. He was always willing to follow Toby's wishes so far as he understood them.

So Toby taught him to watch the garden and keep out roving hens. This pleased Mammy. She began to say a kind word to the hound pup now and then.

Pappy had a fine turnip patch down in No-

End Hollow, which the wild rabbits were rapidly ruining. Soon there would be no greens for the pot or turnips left for winter, Pappy complained.

"We'll see about that, won't we, hound pup?" Toby took his dog hunting in the turnip patch. This scared the rabbits off. Pappy stopped calling the hound pup bad names. He stopped talking of sending him back to Yon-Side.

"Maybe the folks will help me, now," Toby thought, "to think up a suitable name for the hound pup."

Before this could happen, Old Man Trouble caught up with the hound pup again and got him into a bad fix.

Sunday was Big Meeting Day on that side of Little Twin. Once a month the circuit rider came to preach in the little log schoolhouse. It was a great day. Everybody came to hear a fine sermon, meet their friends, and eat a picnic dinner. The Tollivers always went to Big Meeting. Toby liked to watch the big crowds, to hear the people sing, to sample so many kinds of food.

On Saturday, Mammy made gingerbread for the picnic dinner. She was turning her gingerbread out of the pan and dropped a few crumbs. The hound pup dived to get them.

Wham—slam! He ran against Mammy—and the mischief was done. She dropped the ginger-bread on the floor where it broke into little pieces. That very moment Toby entered the

kitchen wth a load of stovewood. "Grab that pup!" yelled Mammy.

Toby grabbed him with one hand—and dropped the load of wood.

Smash—crash! The hound pup hardly knew what had happened, but one thing he understood—this was no place for him! "Boo-oo!" He made for the door. Toby couldn't keep up with him. In the hip-and-hurrah he stumbled over the wood he had dropped. Kersplang—splang! Toby's heels went over his head as he tumbled clear out of the door in a somersault.

By this time, Pappy had heard the big commotion clear out at the barn lot and had come as fast as he could. "Jumping jaybirds!" he whooped. "Whatever has happened?"

"Look-a-there!" wailed Mammy. "Look at my gingerbread there on the floor all broken to pieces. That's what that greedy, good-for-nothing hound pup did. I wish he was back on Yon-Side where he came from."

"That rascally, rowdy hound pup! We ought to get rid of him!" Pappy muttered, eyeing the mess on the kitchen floor.

10

"He meant no harm," Toby said, trying to say a good word for his dog. He looked around for the hound pup now, but he had quickly vanished. Toby guessed he had hidden under the porch. Better let him stay there awhile, Toby thought.

Sunday morning the Tollivers came out of their cabin door dressed up for Big Meeting. All three of them had on their Sunday clothes. Pappy was wearing his new blue britches with shirt and necktie to match. Mammy was wearing her polka-dot calico and stiffly starched, white sunbonnet. Toby had on new overalls and a shirt that was nearly new. But what made him feel fine and fancy was the new rush hat with the bright red band he had bought at Cross Roads Store.

Pappy was carrying on his arm the picnic dinner basket. You could tell by the way he held it that it was a hefty load. Toby's mouth watered when he thought of the good things in that basket: the fried chicken, the biscuit bread, the apple and berry pies, the jelly, the jam, the hard-boiled eggs, the cucumber pickles!

"We've got the best dinner we've ever had

for Big Meeting!" Toby said, sniffing the good smells.

"Oh," wailed Mammy, "if only I hadn't lost my gingerbread! I've always taken gingerbread for Big Meeting dinner. The circuit rider liked it. He says it's like the kind his mother used to make." She gave a sigh as she followed Pappy down the yard walkway. Toby and his hound pup had dashed ahead to the gate.

A frowny look darkened Pappy's face as he spoke, "Reckon we better leave that rowdy-rascal at home."

Mammy agreed, "No telling what'll happen if we take that good-for-nothing along."

"Boo-oo!" barked the hound pup, paying no attention to what was being said about him. He was eager to hurry on.

Toby looked from Pappy to Mammy as he said, "Please, Sir, please, Ma'am, let the hound pup go along. I'll look after him—I'll make him behave. If he doesn't, I'll bring him home."

"All right, that's a bargain," Pappy said. "You're to bring the rowdy rascal home if he acts up."

"When he *starts* to act up," added Mammy, "if it's while the circuit rider's preaching or in the middle of a song."

"Yes, yes!" Toby agreed. He was glad to give this promise. He was certain-sure he could make his pup behave. The dog could lie out in the meetinghouse yard till it was time for dinner— or crawl back under the floor.

Before they sighted the meetinghouse they heard the sound of singing.

"We're not much late," said Toby. "They're singing 'Praise God'—that's always the first song."

"Hurry!" said Pappy.

Outside the meetinghouse was a grove where people ate their picnic dinner. On the limbs of the trees, many baskets were already hung.

Toby spoke up, "Go ahead, Pappy, you and Mammy. I'll find a place for the basket and then I'll come along."

"All right," Pappy agreed. He handed Toby the basket and started for the meetinghouse door. Mammy called back over her shoulder, "Find that hound pup a stay-place and get him settled down before you come in!"

Toby hunted around and soon found a pine limb to hang the dinner basket on. Then he called the hound pup to the tree. "Stay here," he said to him. "Stay here and *watch*. Do you hear, hound pup? Watch the dinner basket."

Toby had taught the hound pup to watch for moles. This trick was much the same. The hound pup sat down under the pine tree with his eyes on the dinner basket which hung out of harm's way, high above his head. Toby gave him a good-bye pat and hurried into the meetinghouse. The preacher was starting his sermon, so Toby sat on the first bench he came to.

He saw Mammy's bonnet away up front and Pappy in the Amen corner, and there was Uncle Tobe from Yon-Side sitting beside him. Toby would go up and speak to him later. He'd want to know if the hound pup was named a *suitable* name! Toby would have to tell the truth that the dog still hadn't a name, and Uncle Tobe would wonder why such a thing had ever been neglected. It would look as if Toby didn't care much for the dog he had given him.

When the last song was called, Toby stood

up and sang "Oh Happy Day!" with the others.
He liked this song and knew it by heart. But
from the woods outside the meetinghouse came
an excited, "Boo-oo-oo!"

Toby ran out of the meetinghouse as quickly

as he could. Then he gave a shout as he saw
what was happening. A thief had the Tolliver's
basket and was making off with it down the
hollow trail. Lickitty-split went his long legs—
but the hound pup was at his heels! "Boo-oo-oo!"
he barked. What a fine race he was having!
More fun than chasing chickens or rabbits!

Toby now was racing, too, faster and faster. Maybe he and the hound pup could get their dinner back.

All of a sudden, the thief gave a shout and dropped the basket. Toby saw the foxy face that gave one backward glance. "Traipsing Tom!" he cried aloud.

Traipsing Tom was a good-for-nothing fellow who, so far as anybody knew, had never done an honest day's work in his life. He spent his time traipsing all over Little Twin Mountain, stealing whatever he could. He had grabbed the Tolliver's basket because it was farthest from the meetinghouse door and out of sight. That's how Toby figured it out as he and the hound pup turned and sat down with the basket. All the food was still there but it was sort of scrambled about.

"Everything's all hunky-dory, thanks to you, hound pup!" he told him.

All-of-a-sudden a notion had come—spang! whang!—into Toby's head. "Whoop-ee! I've thought of a name for you, hound pup—a *suitable* name—Hunkydory!"

Everybody else thought so, too, when they heard the whole story as they ate their picnic feast. "Hurrah for Hunkydory, I say," said Pappy. "He saved our dinner for us. He deserves a treat." Pappy gave him a piece of pie.

"Bless his little heart," said Mammy. "The

next time I bake gingerbread, Hunkydory shall have a slice."

Uncle Tobe was fairly tickled to pieces over his namesake and his dog.

"I'm mighty-much pleased," he said. "You've given your pup a *suitable* name."

Toby hugged his dog. "Seems to me," he said, "that this hound pup has named himself."

Here Comes Step-Along

It was a bright October day in No-End Hollow. Tib and Tildy Messer sat in their cabin door shelling corn. It was the first corn of that year's harvest. When they had a sackful, their father would take it to the mill. Here it would be ground into meal. Later on, their mother would bake it into bread. She might make hoe-cakes, which were round and flat. She might make corn dodgers, round and fat. She might make corn pone, round and even fatter.

"I'll be glad to eat a piece of good old corn

bread for a change," said Tib. "I'm tired of gnawing roas'in' ears in place of bread."

"Me, too," his sister agreed. "A piece of corn bread and butter will be mighty tasty."

In the lean-to kitchen they could hear their mother churning and singing this old song:

> Come, butter come!
> Come butter, come!
> Peter at the gate,
> Wants a buttered cake.
> Come butter, come!

"I wonder who Peter is," Tib said to his sister.

"It couldn't be the circuit rider. His first name is John," Tildy said thoughtfully.

"And it isn't the peddler," said Tib, "his name is Step-Along."

"That's not his sure-enough name," said Tildy. "That's just his nickname."

"I know that," said her brother, "and I know how the peddler got that name. When folks ask him to stay awhile longer, he always says, 'I must step along.'"

24

"I know that as well as you," said Tildy.

Then she jumped up from the cabin doorstep, spilling her lapful of corn.

"Look-a-yonder!" she cried. "Look down the hollow! There comes somebody with a pack—and it's bound to be Step-Along!"

Tib jumped up with his pan of corn. He managed not to spill it. He looked down No-End Hollow trail.

"Yes, yes, it's Step-Along, sure as shooting," he agreed.

From the kitchen their mother heard them and came to see what they were shouting about.

"Here comes Step-Along!" Tib and Tildy told her.

Mr. Messer was working at the barn. It was not far from the cabin. He came out and saw his family in the door of the house.

"Are you-all calling me?" he asked.

"Here comes Step-Along!" everyone answered.

By this time the peddler was near enough to hear their greeting:

"Howdy, Step-Along!"

"Howdy, folks!" he called back.

Tib and Tildy ran down the trail to meet him.

"You look just about tuckered out," Mr. Messer said.

"No-End Hollow trail seems steeper everytime I climb it. I guess it's because I'm getting older," Step-Along sighed.

"What you need is a good lie-down here and now," Mrs. Messer told him. "I'll make you up a good pallet bed in a shady corner of the yard. You can take a nap and rest your bones till I fix you a bite of dinner. We'll have something tasty for you by and by."

"I won't say no," Step-Along said. "A rest and a bite of food are just what I need."

While the peddler took his rest, the Messers all got busy. Tib and Tildy hurried to finish shelling the corn. Mr. Messer poured it into a sack and took it to the mill down the hollow. There it was quickly ground into meal. As soon as he returned, Mrs. Messer made it into a fine corn pone. By the time that dinner was ready, Step-Along had awakened from his nap.

"I feel better," he declared, "but I do feel hungry."

"There's new corn pone," Tib told Step-Along.

"And fresh butter," said Tildy.

"And a pot of strengthy sassafras tea," Mrs. Messer smiled.

"What are we waiting for?" Mr. Messer cried. "Let's set our feet under the table." And everyone did just that.

"As soon as dinner is over, maybe Step-Along will open his pack," Tib whispered to Tildy.

"I do hope so," she whispered back.

Mrs. Messer shook her head at them, "No whispering at the table. Remember your manners now."

Perhaps the peddler had heard Tib and Tildy. As soon as dinner was over he went to his pack and opened it. Then he poured out its treasure on the cabin floor. Packets of shiny needles and pins, rolls of bright ribbon, gay handkerchiefs, strings of glittering beads, pocket knives, shoestrings, neckties—all these and many more treasures. What a sight it was!

"Look at that knife," Tib whispered to Tildy.

"Look at that red ribbon," said Tildy. They wanted these things very much, but they had

no money to buy them—not one penny. They would have no money of their own until next summer, when they could pick and sell huckleberries. That was a long, long time away, but it was fun to see all these pretty things anyway.

"Maybe next time you come we'll be able to buy something," Mr. Messer said.

"Yes, I hope so," his wife added.

Then Step-Along told the sad news he had been waiting to tell them.

"This may be my last trip," he said. "I guess I'm getting too old for the job. It was hard climbing that trail today. I needed a rest pretty bad by the time I got here. Now I feel a lot better, thanks to you good people, but I must be stepping along. Got to climb the trail to the mountain top and go down the other side."

Tib said, "I could help you with your pack to the top of the mountain."

"I could help, too," Tildy added.

But Step-Along shook his head. "It's too heavy a load for either one of you to carry."

"We could tote it together," Tib said. "We could tote it on a stick between us."

"The way we do a basket of corn," Tildy explained.

"I reckon you two could manage it that way," said their father.

This plan worked out very well. With the load between them, Tib and Tildy didn't find the pack too heavy. They kept ahead of the old peddler clear to the top of the trail. Step-Along took the pack now. He untied the strings.

"Pick yourselves a gift apiece," he told them. "It will be a thank-you present for helping me with my load."

Tib and Tildy looked at each other. They looked up at the peddler.

"You don't have to pay us," Tib said, "for a little old thing like that."

"We *wanted* to help you, Step-Along," Tildy said.

"I know you did," said the peddler. "I know you wanted to help me—and you certainly helped me a lot. I appreciate your kindness. That's why I want to give you a thank-gift. Go ahead," he added, "pick out something you like."

Tib picked out a knife with two blades.

"Thank you mighty much," he said. "I've always wanted a knife of my own."

Tildy selected a yard roll of beautiful, bright blue ribbon. This would make a headband for her curly, red hair, with a big bow on top.

"Thank you. Oh, thank you!" She danced up and down, waving the ribbon in the air. "I won't wear this everyday. I'll save it for Sunday."

Step-Along re-tied his pack and slung it across his shoulder. He looked at the sun. "It's getting late. I must step along," he said.

"When will you be back?" they asked him.

"I don't know exactly," the peddler replied. "A while ago, I thought that this might be my very last trip, but I think I can keep on with my job if you will help me carry my load up the steepest part of No-End Hollow trail."

"Yes. Oh, yes!"

"We will, we will," the children shouted together.

"It's a bargain then," the peddler said, and he started to step along the trail that wound down to the foot of the mountain.

Tib and Tildy watched him go out of sight. Then, holding their new treasures, they raced down the trail toward home.

A Good Stay-Place

Jimmy Greer leaned on his hoe in the middle of a potato row. He pushed back his ragged, old, straw hat and looked up at the sky. By the sun's place over Little Twin Mountain, he guessed the time to be about ten o'clock. Two more long, hot hours of hard work digging potatoes must pass till he could go in for dinner. There would be only black-eyed peas and corn pone, but most any food tastes good to a ten-year-old boy who has worked from sun-up till the middle of the morning.

"Get on with that hoe, boy!" came a loud

shout from the hill, where Si Clevenger sat in the shade of a tree in his apple orchard and smoked his pipe. He liked to keep an eye on whoever he had working for him.

"I don't pay folks I hire for loafing on the job," he often said.

Of course, he didn't pay Jimmy Greer for his work—not a penny in money. He claimed that he paid him more than he was worth in his board and keep. He had taken him in after the death of Jimmy's father the year before. Until that time, the Greers had lived in a little tenant shack on Si Clevenger's place. The only thing they had ever owned that had much value was Samson, a mule. Samson had once been very strong and had helped the Greers to make a living. He was Jimmy's special pet. Samson was old now, and not able to work as well as he once did. Only last night, Si Clevenger had said he aimed to get rid of him.

"I'll sell him and put the money into the price of another mule," he had told Jimmy. "I need a young mule that's worth his feed. That lazy old Samson's not worth shucks."

"He is, too!" Jimmy had flared up. "Samson's not a bit lazy. He works as well as he can, and you can't sell him. He's *my* mule!"

"Don't sass me, boy!" Old Si had cried, with a blow that sent the boy reeling. "I took that mule on your daddy's debts. I've told you that before."

Jimmy hadn't dared to say anything more, but he knew that this was not true. His father had always bragged, even when times were hardest, that he didn't owe a penny to any man.

All this was going through Jimmy's mind as he went on digging potatoes. The sharp *clink-clank* of the hoe kept time to his troubled thoughts.

"Gee! Haw!" came the voice of a man who was plowing farther down the hollow. Jimmy couldn't see him, but he knew who the plowman was. It was Mr. Hacker, a neighbor who had come over that morning to borrow Samson for a morning's work.

"I'd like to try him out and see if he's worth anything." Jimmy had overheard this tag-end of conversation between Mr. Hacker and Old Si.

Mr. Hacker, Jimmy understood, was as mean-minded and heavy-handed as Old Si was. He couldn't stand to think of Samson falling into his hands. He was so troubled over Samson's fate that he had little appetite for dinner.

Old Si eyed the black-eyed peas and corn pone on Jimmy's plate. "You don't feel sick, do you, boy?" he asked. "Have you got a pain somewhere?" His eyes and voice were anxious.

Jimmy shook his head. He couldn't explain.

"Don't you get sick, boy," said Old Si. "Don't you go and get sick on me, now, with so much work to be done. You've got to earn your board and keep."

Old Si said this at least once a day. This taunt always made Jimmy angry, but he dared not answer. Before he went back to his work, he ran to the barn to have a look at his mule. Samson was standing with his head hunched over a manger from which the feed had disappeared.

"You're still hungry, old boy, I know," Jimmy said. He rubbed him gently. "Never mind, I'll be back tonight to slip you some corn."

"Hee-haw!" Samson threw up his head as if he understood this promise.

Jimmy heard footsteps and voices outside. He darted up a ladder into the hayloft that was over the stall. Old Si would have a fit if he found him idle here in the barn. It was easy for Jimmy to hear the voices below.

"I'll buy the old plug if you'll sell him for twenty-five dollars. I doubt if he lives long

enough to be worth that." Mr. Hacker was speaking. Jimmy waited for Old Si's answer.

"Well—Well, I'll think about your offer. I always like to think about a trade overnight. Come back and see me in the morning. If somebody else hasn't bought the mule before then, we might make a deal."

Mr. Hacker's loud laugh ended in a snort. "I reckon I don't have to worry about losing the old mule," he answered.

Old Si laughed with him as they walked away. Neither one of them would have laughed if they could have known the plan that had popped all-of-a-sudden into Jimmy Greer's head.

It was late in the morning of the next day when Jimmy Greer came riding out of No-End Hollow trail to the other side of Little Twin. He and Samson had slipped away around midnight, after Old Si was fast asleep. Jimmy was tired from the long trip and so, he knew, was Samson. Far back on the trail they had eaten the little food they had—a hunk of bread and a few ears of corn.

Jimmy had never been to this side of Little Twin Mountain. At every turn of the trail, he looked anxiously ahead. He hoped before long to come in sight of a cabin, where they could stop and rest and get some food. It wouldn't be begging. No, sir-ee! He wouldn't ask a bite for nothing, but most anybody ought to have a little work for a boy and mule. Of course, what he and Samson needed most was a home, a sure-enough stay-place, where they could earn their board and keep.

A fearful thought had followed him all the way to this side of the mountain. What would Old Si do when he found him gone? Would he follow him and his mule clear over to Near-Side? He had no rightful claim on him or his mule, but Old Si was a crafty fellow. There was no telling what he might do. The farther away they were from Old Si, the better it would be for them.

"Get up, Samson! We better hip-and-hurry on," he told his mule.

Around the next turn in the trail, a hound pup dashed out on them.

"Boo-oo-oo!" he barked, darting under the mule's legs. Samson was so frightened by the hound pup that he started a mad dance. Jimmy slid first one way and then the other.

"Whoa, Samson, whoa!" he cried.

A tow-headed boy about Jimmy's age hurried up. "Come here! Come here, Snapper!" he yelled.

The hound pup obeyed. He came with his tail

a-wag, as if to say, "Don't scold me. It was all in fun."

"You behave yourself, now," his master told him. "Get behind me and stay there, Snapper."

Jimmy laughed, "That's a good name for that dog! The way he acted, seemed like he wanted to snap me up and Samson, too."

The other boy grinned, "It's a habit o' his. Snaps like a turtle. That's how he got his name when he was a little pup. But except for his manners, he's a mighty fine dog."

"He looks like a fine dog," said Jimmy, then his face sobered. "I had a pup, but Old Si Clevenger gave him away—said he ate too much."

The other boy said, "I never heard tell of a man so mean and stingy."

"Well, he was—and he is!" said Jimmy. "I reckon Old Si is the meanest, stingiest man on Yon-Side. That's why I've left him for good. Wish I'd done it sooner, right after my pappy died, but Old Si offered me a home—said he would look after me. All he wanted was a work-hand and a mule."

"Where are you headed for?" the other boy asked.

"A stay-place," Jimmy answered. "A good stay-place for me and Samson. A place where we can earn our way. We both know how to work."

"You ought to go home with me," said the other boy. "I'd like mighty-much to have a partner help me with the work. My grandpappy has been laid up a whole month with rheumatism. I can't do half of all there is to do— there's work at the house, work at the barn, work in the fields and garden. I reckon my folks would be tickled to have you tarry with us. I know I would, certain-sure."

Jimmy nodded, "I might do that, but what about my mule?"

The other boy grinned, "My mule, Dilly-dolly, is an awful slowpoke. I reckon he would like to have a partner, too."

Jimmy slipped off Samson's back. "This mule won't carry double, so I'll mosey along with you."

Then he stopped stock-still and chuckled, "I know the name of your pup, you know the name

of my mule, but we don't know each other's name—mine is Jimmy Greer."

"Mine's Davy Carr," the other boy replied.

They had come to a little crossroads store. Davy said, "I've got to stop here and get a bottle of 'Pain Killer' for my grandpappy's rheumatism."

Jimmy waited till Davy came back, then they went along together. Jimmy led Samson. Snapper trotted behind in a peaceable way.

Grandmammy Carr stood in the doorway to welcome them as they came up. She smiled at Jimmy and shook hands with him.

"Come in and make yourself at home," she said.

How good these words of welcome sounded to Jimmy!

Grandpappy called from his chair in a corner, "Howdy! Come in! Come in!"

A little later at the dinner table, Jimmy told them all the story of his life on Yon-Side with Old Si Clevenger.

Grandmammy Carr listened with a sigh and wiped her eyes on her apron. Grandpappy

growled, "I've heard about that mean old man.
He would skin a gnat for its hide and tallow—
that's what I've heard about him. But don't you
worry about Old Si. You can bet he'll run
into trouble if he comes over here after you
or your mule."

"Grandpappy's a deputy sheriff," Davy said
proudly. "He can make bad folks behave."

48

"Yes, you are safe with us," Grandmammy said, patting Jimmy's shoulder. "You need us, and we need you." She gave him a piece of hot corn pone already buttered.

"Mighty-much obliged," said Jimmy.

He was thankful for more than the food. He was happy that he had found a good stay-place for himself and Samson, too.

Jumping Johnny

A shooting star fell over No-End Hollow the night that Johnny Jones was born.

"That is a certain-sure sign that he will be a wonder boy," said the Good Witch Woman on Far-Side.

Everyone waited to see what would happen. They didn't have to wait long. One day, while his mammy was rocking his cradle, Johnny kicked the covers off and jumped out onto the floor.

His mammy jumped right after him, yelling in distress:

"Look out, look out, Johnny Jones!
Ef you jump like that,
You'll break your bones!"

She grabbed him up and looked him over for bumps and bruises. Johnny didn't cry. He laughed up at her and kept jumping in her lap.

She had to call Pappy Jones to hold him while she greased him with goose grease.

"This will keep him from getting sore," she said.

But Johnny didn't seem to like this a bit. He jumped so hard he got away from Pappy. This time he sailed out the cabin door and landed in the front yard. Both his parents dashed after him.

"He'll be killed, certain-sure!" cried Mammy.

But by great good luck, Johnny had landed in the middle of a peony patch which had kept the fall from hurting him. The flowers were broken but not Johnny's bones. Pappy felt him all over.

"He's all right, I reckon," he said to Mammy. "What a jumper! Reckon we'll have to call him Jumping Johnny."

As time went by, the little boy did his best to live up to his name.

The day that he was six years old, his mammy had a notion. "This morning," she said, "I shall bake you a big, fancy-fine birthday cake."

"How big?" Jumping Johnny asked. He very seldom had cake to eat.

"Six layers high," his mammy replied, "because you are six years old today."

"With huckleberry jam for filling?" he asked.

"Yes," promised his mammy. She knew that this was her little boy's favorite kind of jam.

"Whoopee!" he yelled, jumping till his head nearly hit the ceiling. This would be the very finest birthday cake he had ever had.

But when Mammy Jones went to make the cake, she found the egg basket empty.

"Run to the barn," she told her son, "and bring me six eggs."

The boy came back empty handed. "I can't find an egg," he said sadly. "Some varmint has raided all the nests. There's nothing left but the shells." He was almost crying, but his mammy had another notion.

"Run down the hollow to Aunt Debbie Dickerson's. She has a big flock of chickens. She's sure to have plenty of eggs. Borrow half-a-dozen from her, but go in a hip-and-hurry, and come back the same way if you want that birthday cake for dinner."

"Yes, ma'am, I will," promised Johnny.

He started down the hollow toward Aunt Debbie Dickerson's, but he didn't follow the trail. He made his trip more quickly by going a shorter way. A very hard, rough way it was, but Jumping Johnny never minded. Leaping over bushes, rocks, and stumps was nothing but fun for him.

The last leap he made took him over a fence that went around the barnyard. Here Aunt Debbie, with a basket of corn, was feeding her big flock of chickens. Jumping Johnny landed right in the middle of them. You never in all your life heard such a commotion. The chickens squawked as if scared to death and flew this way and that. Some landed on the barn roof, some hid in the fence corners, some ran for the woods.

Aunt Debbie wrung her hands and scolded, "What a mean thing to do! You're a rapscallion, Jumping Johnny."

"I'm sorry, Aunt Debbie," the boy said. "I didn't mean to do that. I just came to borrow some eggs for my birthday cake."

As the boy explained, Aunt Debbie smiled.

She was now in a better humor. "If the eggs are needed," she said, "for a birthday cake, I'll *give* them to you. You needn't pay them back. But first," she added, "you must find all my chickens, and get them back in the barn lot."

"Yes, Ma'am, I will," he said; and he did. It took him a good while to round up the whole flock.

When at last he got home with the eggs, his mammy said, "What took you so long?"

Jumping Johnny explained. When his mammy understood what had happened, she didn't scold him.

"But it's too late, now, to make a cake in time for dinner," she said.

"What about supper?" Jumping Johnny asked. "It would be just as good for supper."

And it was, for it was a beautiful cake—six layers high with lots of huckleberry jam filling. Jumping Johnny liked it so much he ate three pieces of it!

That fall, Jumping Johnny started to school. At first, his mammy was worried because the school was at least five miles away.

"It's too far for a six-year-old," she said to Pappy Jones.

"It would be too far for any other six-year-old," Pappy said, "but not for a fellow like our Jumping Johnny. He'll get there and back with no trouble at all."

Pappy was right. The very first day Jumping Johnny went to school, he got there ahead of the other pupils and the teacher. He did this every day. He got home in good time, too. The trip never seemed to tire him.

Jumping Johnny liked school very much. The thing he liked most about it was recess. It was fun to play games in the big shady schoolyard. The other children soon learned that Jumping Johnny was good at "For Race," "Tag," and "Whoopee Hide." He nearly always won in running games on account of his limber legs.

But his legs got him into trouble one time. Mr. Rector, the teacher, caught him jumping in and out of a window one afternoon. He was doing it just for fun, he explained. But this didn't suit Mr. Rector, who went to the blackboard and wrote these lines:

"Windows are made for looking through,
  Not for jumping out—this means *you*."

He made Jumping Johnny write this twenty-five times. It took a long while to do it, and there was no playtime for him that afternoon.

As Jumping Johnny grew older, his folks and friends were worried about him. There were certain ordinary jobs that he couldn't or wouldn't do very well. He was no good at chopping wood, hoeing in the garden, mending a fence, or milking a cow. Jumping Johnny wouldn't stick to such a job long enough to finish it. He would all of a sudden get restless and go leaping and lopping off somewhere else. His parents tried to be patient.

"Maybe our boy will outgrow his heedless way," they said.

The neighbors shook their heads. "That Jumping Johnny is turning out a good-for-nothing. He'll never earn his salt."

But in spite of their harsh opinions of Jumping Johnny, they found him useful in some ways. He came in handy to go for the herb doctor on Yon-

Side. He was always willing to take a message to distant kin. He carried news of play-parties in the winter and picnics in the summer. Yes, Jumping Johnny was a help sometimes. That could not be denied, but he never earned a cent for himself. He never charged the neighbors for going on errands for them, no matter how far. His only pay was, "Much obliged," or "Thanks to you, Jumping Johnny." Sometimes, he didn't get this. Then something happened to make them change their minds.

One day, Jumping Johnny went on a trip to Slab Town, the county seat, and came back with big news. A circus was coming next week. It was almost beyond believing.

"Are you sure?" everyone asked Jumping Johnny. "Are you *certain-sure?*" No one on Near-Side and Far had ever been to a circus.

"Yes," Jumping Johnny told them, "I am certain-sure."

He unrolled a poster before their eyes. "Look at this! Look at this!" he told them. "A man in the county seat gave me this to tote around and show."

As Jumping Johnny held up the poster, he read what was printed on it in big, red letters:

COME ONE! COME ALL!
SEE THE GREATEST SHOW ON EARTH!
LIONS! ELEPHANTS!
A FIRE-EATING MAN!
AND MANY MORE WONDERS
ADMISSION $1.00

"It must be a mighty-fine show to be worth a whole dollar," somebody said, "and if I have a dollar by next week, I aim to go."

Jumping Johnny remembered something then. He pulled a dollar from his pocket and showed it to everyone standing around.

"Where—?"

"How—?"

"Who—?" everyone wanted to know. Nobody could ever remember seeing Jumping Johnny with a dollar before.

Now he explained that this was pay for advertising the circus on this side of the mountain.

"A dollar just for telling a piece of news!"

"It's almost past believing!" People said all this and more, but Jumping Johnny had the dollar to prove what he said.

A good many folks from Near-Side and Far went to the circus at Slab Town. Those who had to stay at home heard about the wonderful show. It had been worth going to see. It was something to tell about.

After this, Jumping Johnny became a most important person. He had been hired by the head circus man to carry the wonderful news of the wonderful show. He had earned cash money—a whole dollar! No longer would Jumping Johnny be asked to do errands for nothing. Granny Owens gave him a goosefeather pillow for going for the herb doctor. He was rewarded with apple pies and cakes and gingerbread. Sometimes, he brought home a chicken for the pot or a basket of extra-fine potatoes.

Thanks to Jumping Johnny, the Jones family fared very well, indeed. Pappy Jones and Mammy Jones never got tired of bragging about him.

"That boy," they would say, "has always known how to use his legs."

MAY JUSTUS has lived most of her life in the region of the Great Smoky Mountains, the scene of many of her numerous books. She says, "I've never lived long in any city or town, for I feel at home only in the mountains." Her home is a little gray house, next to the old school-ground where once stood the school where she taught for many years. After 25 years, she retired from teaching to devote all her time to writing. Many of Miss Justus' stories are based on her own experiences as a little girl or on the folktales and folk songs her mother passed on to her. This is her second book for Garrard following *It Happened In No-End Hollow*. In these and her many other books, among which have been several award winners, she shares, with children all over the world, the Tennessee folklore she knows and loves.

HERMAN B. VESTAL loves both painting and the sea. Before studying art at the National Academy of Design and Pratt Institute, he went to sea in the Merchant Marine. During World War II he served in the Coast Guard as a combat artist. His assignments included recording the Normandy landing and the invasion of Iwo Jima. Today, his interest in the sea continues through his hobby — sailboat racing. Primarily a book illustrator, Mr. Vestal also enjoys doing watercolors and is a member of the American Watercolor Society. Mr. Vestal, his wife, and son live in Little Silver, New Jersey.